The Newbies

Story and Pictures by
Peter Catalanotto

A Richard Jackson Book
Atheneum Books for Young Readers
New York London Toronto Sydney New Delhi atheneum

To Will

Thanks to Marcella for her wonderful photos;
thanks also to Scott, Sarah, and especially Silas.

A atheneum ATHENEUM BOOKS FOR YOUNG READERS
An imprint of Simon & Schuster Children's Publishing Division • 1230 Avenue of the Americas, New York, New York 10020 • Copyright © 2015 by Peter Catalanotto • All rights reserved, including the right of reproduction in whole or in part in any form. • ATHENEUM BOOKS FOR YOUNG READERS is a registered trademark of Simon & Schuster, Inc. • Atheneum logo is a trademark of Simon & Schuster, Inc. • For information about special discounts for bulk purchases, please contact Simon & Schuster Special Sales at 1-866-506-1949 or business@simonandschuster.com. • The Simon & Schuster Speakers Bureau can bring authors to your live event. For more information or to book an event, contact the Simon & Schuster Speakers Bureau at 1-866-248-3049 or visit our website at www.simonspeakers.com. • Book design by Lauren Rille • The text for this book is set in Clarendon LT Std. • The illustrations for this book are rendered in watercolor. • Manufactured in China • 0415 SCP • First Edition • 10 9 8 7 6 5 4 3 2 1 • Library of Congress Cataloging-in-Publication Data • Catalanotto, Peter. • Newbies / Peter Catalanotto ; illustrated by Peter Catalanotto.—First edition. • p. cm • "A Richard Jackson Book." • Summary: A boy whose parents are preoccupied with preparations for a new baby imagines what life would be like if he could have new parents. • ISBN 978-1-4814-1892-8 (hardcover)—ISBN 978-1-4814-1893-5 (eBook) • [1. Parent and child—Fiction.] I. Catalanotto, Peter, illustrator. II. Title. • PZ7.C26878New 2015 • [E]—dc23 • 2013047676

Every Saturday I choose
 the ears for my pancakes.
"Rabbit ears," Dad says,
"one floppy, one straight."
"Can we play soccer after?" I ask.

"Not today," Dad says.
 "I'm painting the nursery.
 The new baby will be here soon."

"Can I help?"

"We'll see," Dad says. The doorbell rings.

"Hello," says a woman. "We have information
for new parents. We heard there's a baby coming."

"But we're not new parents," Dad says.

The couple looks at me.

"Our pamphlet might be useful," says the man.

"Okay," Dad says. "Thank you for stopping by."

He drops the pamphlet on the table.

I ask Mom if we can make a tent.
"Maybe later," she says. "The baby was kicking
all night. I'm tired."
"Ummm . . . Tell me a story? About when I was little!"
"After I rest, sweetie," Mom says.

"Are you hungry?" Dad asks Mom.
"I am," she says, "but I really need to lie down."

I pick up the pamphlet. It says "New Parents."

I tell Mom and Dad I need to talk to them.

"You both have been very busy and tired lately."

The doorbell rings. "Expecting someone?" Dad asks.

"Yes," I say. "Come in!"

My new parents enter the house. "Hello. We're the Newbies."

I say to Mom and Dad, "You are my first parents
and you will always be special to me. You know that I love you."

I turn to my new parents.

"Let's go!"

My new parents play soccer with me.
We make a huge tent in the backyard.
We fly my kite and climb trees.

At lunch New Mom makes me a peanut butter
and banana sandwich. She cuts it into four squares.
I tell her I like triangles. She says it will taste the same.
It doesn't, but that's okay.

After lunch
we ride bikes to Jimmy's.
I get a double scoop
chocolate cone.

"Aren't you going to make me
look behind me, so you can sneak
some of mine?"

"No," says New Dad.
"I have my own ice cream."

Back home we play hide-and-seek.

I hide, but my new parents find me right away.

"You're supposed to look

in lots of other places first!

Like under the flowerpots!

Then you look in the garden hose

and I turn on the water!"

New Mom and New Dad look at each other.

"Never mind," I say.

"Can I invite some friends over?"

"Yes," says New Mom.

We play kickball, tag,
and capture the flag.

New Mom makes cookies
and lemonade.

After my friends leave, New Dad asks
if I want to sleep in the tent tonight.
"Yes!"
"What would you like for dinner?" New Mom asks.
"Pancakes!" I say. "With puppy ears!"

"Okay," she says. "Go wash up and bring back
some clean socks."

Upstairs, I wash my hands
and grab socks from my room.
When I sit at the table,
New Dad places a plate in front of me.
Three round pancakes.

New Mom puts the socks on my ears.

"Puppy ears!" she cries.

"The ears are supposed to go on the pancakes," I say.

"Never put socks on pancakes,"
 New Dad says. "That's disgusting."
"But . . ."
"Never," he repeats.

In front of the tent, New Dad makes a fire.

"Let's tell stories," says New Mom. "What kind would you like?"

"One about me . . . when I was little."

New Dad looks at New Mom.

"When you were little," New Mom says, "ummm . . ."

"You couldn't talk," New Dad says.

"That's right!" New Mom says. "And you couldn't walk, either!" They smile.

I stand up. "Thank you for a wonderful day."

"You going to eat
   your rabbit ears?"

"Huh?" I look up at Dad.

"I'm taking this to Mom," he says.

"Wait for me!"

Dad tells Mom
that I want to help
paint the nursery.

She smiles.

"The last time you helped Dad,
you tipped your container
and the paint poured into your pocket.
When you saw your cup was empty,
Dad had to explain what happened.
You didn't believe him
so you stuck your hand in your pocket."

"Really?" I ask.

"Really," Mom says.

I look at Dad.
He opens
the closet door.
There's a
blue handprint
and my name.

"Tell me again," I say.